Miss Malarkey Doesn't Live in Room 10

Judy Finchler

Illustrations by Kevin O'Malley

Walker and Company
New York

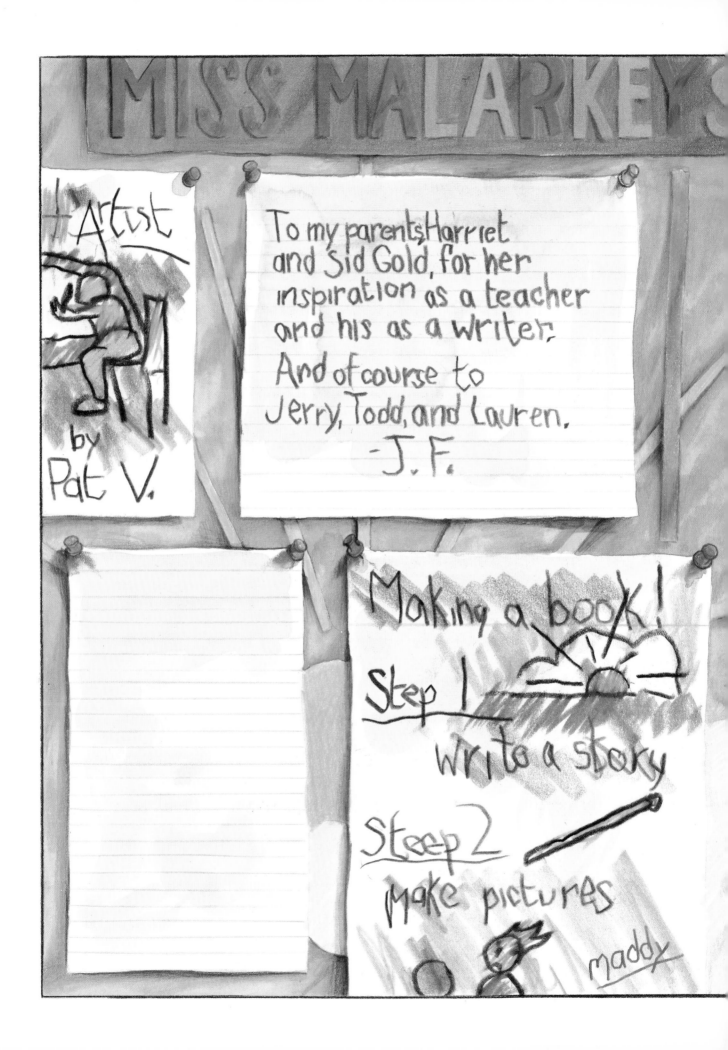

CLASS PROJECTS

Making a Book Dan V, editor

agent & arist drawrings editor Book

First u git a store. Thn u rite Thn u mak pechers

How you m a pictu by shawr

Get so paper

This is a Book

1 ☐ ☐

Draw

R Write

This book is for

① Connor
② Noah   -K.O.

I know that Miss Malarkey, my teacher, lives right here at school in Room 10.

That's where she marks our papers
and puts up all the next day's work.

She eats dinner in the cafeteria, and
her table is always the best.

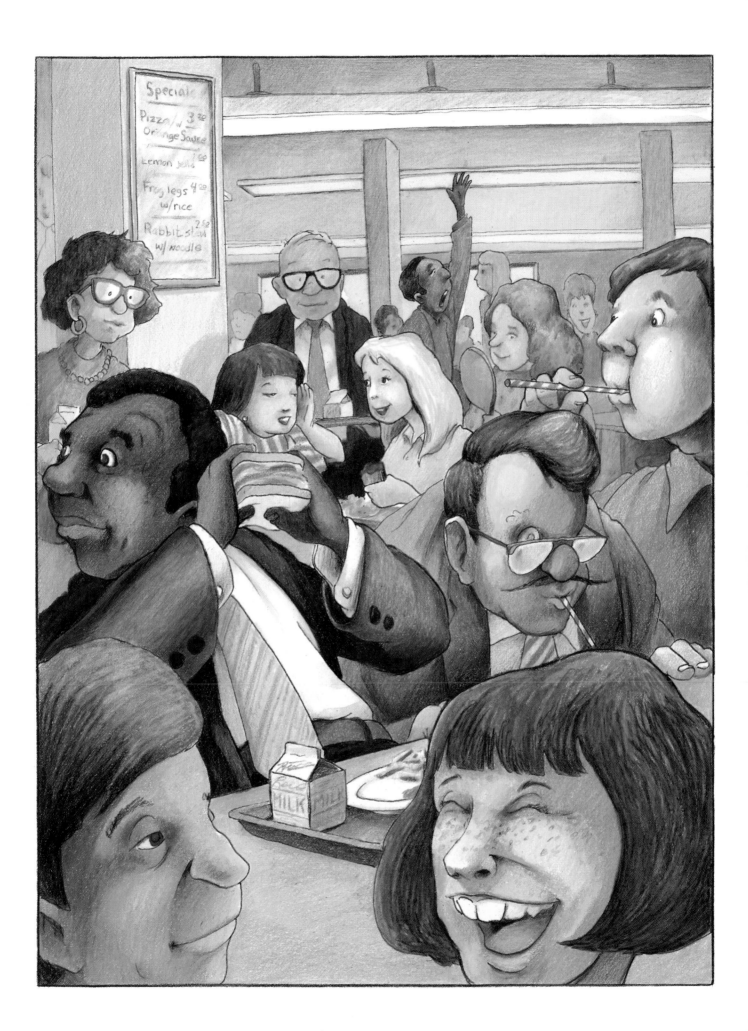

After dinner she plays in the gym with the other teachers. And she never forgets her gym clothes.

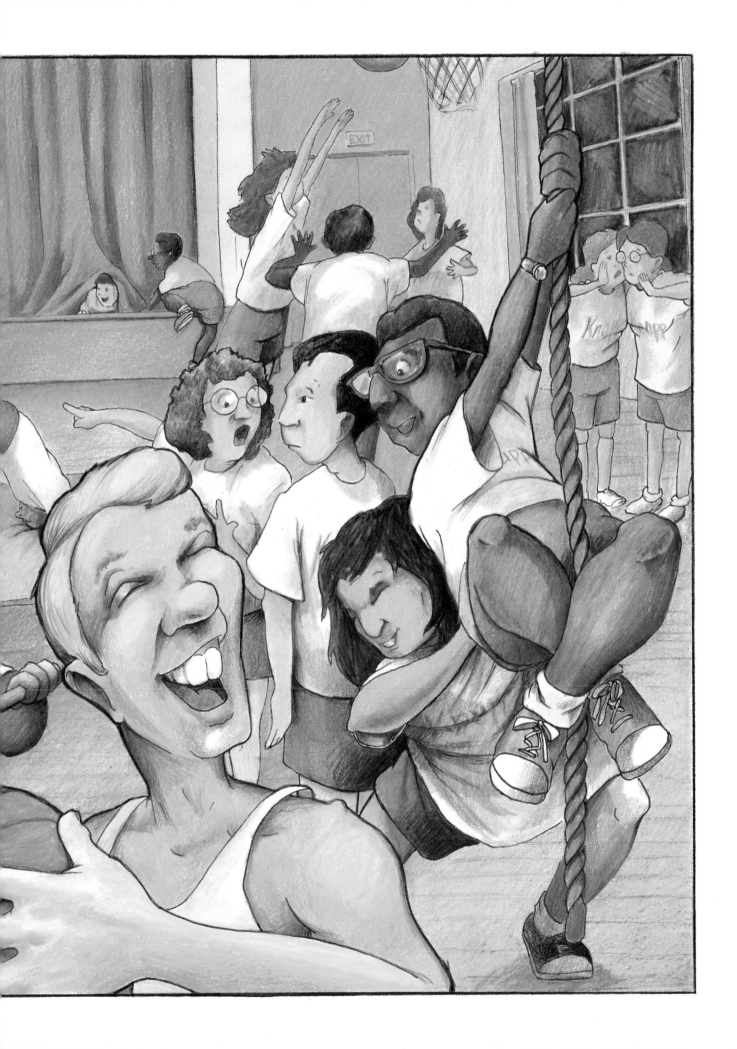

I wonder what the Teachers' Room looks like. That must be where they all sleep. No wonder kids aren't allowed in there. I'm sure teachers don't want us to see their messy room.

Room 10 is a great place to live. It's near the best water fountain in the whole school—the only one that squirts up lots of water.

And the Boys' Room is right across
the hall. . . . Oops!—I mean the Girls'
Room isn't too far away, either.

But last week Miss Malarkey came to our apartment house with a mountain of boxes.

Mom says she's going to live *here* now!

A few days ago when Mom and I
baked cookies, she asked me to bring
some upstairs to Miss Malarkey. I told
her I needed a pass.

Before I knocked, I spit out my gum.

When she opened the
door, she gave me a
great big hug. Then
I saw her feet!
Miss Malarkey had no
shoes on or socks or
even slippers! I could
see Miss Malarkey's
toenails and they
were red—bright red!

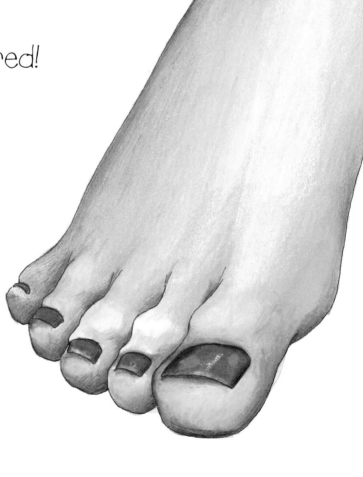

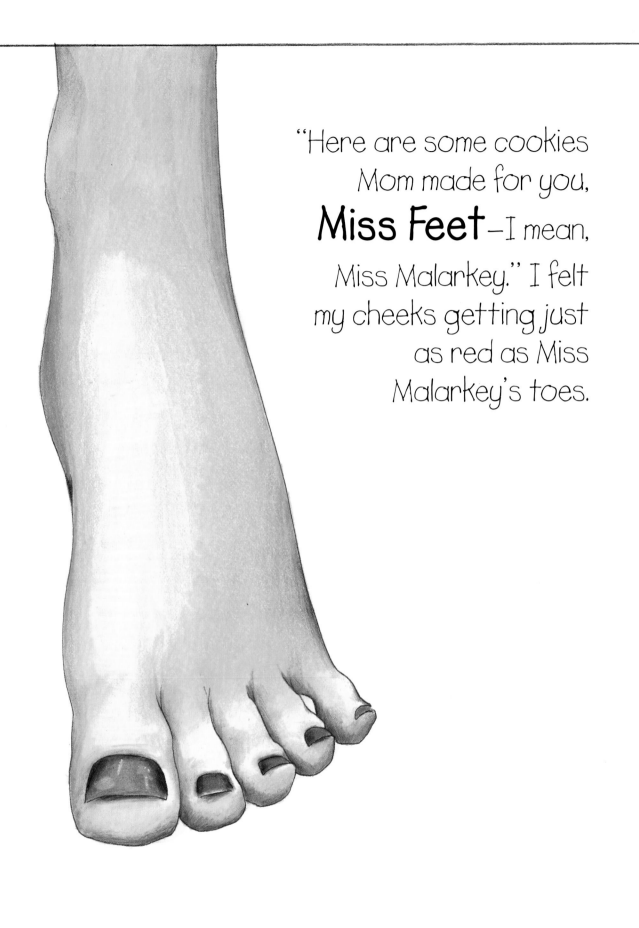

"Here are some cookies Mom made for you, **Miss Feet**—I mean, Miss Malarkey." I felt my cheeks getting just as red as Miss Malarkey's toes.

That very same day I spotted her
throwing out the garbage.

She never does that at school!

On Saturday I saw some people going
into Miss Malarkey's apartment. She
was having a party.
And it wasn't even someone in the
class's birthday!

I told everyone in my class that our teacher doesn't live in Room 10. Some of them still didn't believe me. So I showed them.

I like having Miss Malarkey live in the same apartment house as me. But I won't see her so much when I go to second grade.

Next year I'll have
Mrs. Boba. Mrs. Boba
doesn't live in my
building.

Miss Malarkey Won't Be in Today

Miss Malarkey
Won't Be in Today

Judy Finchler

Illustrations by Kevin O'Malley

Walker & Company ☀ New York

I couldn't go to school this morning,
not with a fever of **103.2.**

I had to call Principal Wiggins.

Principal Wiggins doesn't *like* it
when a teacher calls in sick.

Then he has to find a substitute.

He hates finding substitutes.

Oh,

and the last substitute he found

for Mrs. Boba's class didn't exactly work out.

My poor class!

What if he called Mr. Doberman?

That guy is so tough he even scares me.

Or he might have called Mrs. Ungerware.

The kids call her Mrs. *Underwear.*

Once my kids start laughing, they'll never stop.

Mrs. *Underwear* won't be able

to get anything done.

Oh, I hope he didn't call Mr. Lemonjello.

Mr. Lemonjello

is

such a

n e r v o u s

man.

Sometimes my kids

can be a handful.

He'll be scared **stiff** if they let
the iguana
out of its
cage.

He'll never be able to
handle them in music class.
They'll crank up the
volume.

They'll dance on the desks.
They'll swing from the lights.

And then they'll all ask to go to the bathroom at the same time.

At the same time!

I have to get to school.

Right now!

Everyone looks okay.

Better than I imagined.

Better behaved than they are for me?

Oh, my class!

Oh, the bell!

Oh, my head!

"Miss Malarkey, where were you today?"
"Did Mr. Wiggins make you sit out here?"

"Oh, no. I didn't feel very well today,
but I've been worried sick about everybody."

"We're fine, but you look terrible."
"Feel her head. Maybe she needs an ice pack."
"Let's take her to the nurse in case
she needs to throw up."

"*Don't worry,* Miss Malarkey.
You just stay home and rest up."

"And if Mrs. Berpur is
our teacher tomorrow,
we'll take care of everything."

Oh no, not Ima Berpur!

TESTING MISS MALARKEY

Judy Finchler

Illustrations by **Kevin O'Malley**

WALKER & COMPANY ✳ NEW YORK

Miss Malarkey is a good teacher. Usually she's really nice. But a couple of weeks ago she started acting a little weird. She started talking about THE TEST: The Instructional Performance Through Understanding test. I think Miss Malarkey said it was called the "I.P.T.U." test.

But Miss Malarkey said THE TEST wasn't that important. She said it wouldn't affect our report cards. It wouldn't mean extra homework. And if we didn't do well, we'd still go on to the next grade.

At recess we played Multiplication Mambo. Each class got new CD roms called "There's Something About Decimals." After lunch we played Funny Phonics. Miss Malarkey said you never know what's going to be on THE TEST.

The closer we got to "THE TEST DAY," the weirder things got. When I brought the attendance sheets to the office, I heard Principal Wiggins yelling about pencils.

The cafeteria lady, Mrs. Slopdown, took away the potato chips and served only fish.

In art we each made posters about THE TEST. Mrs. Magenta

also showed us how to color in all those little circles they put

on tests.

During gym we didn't play baseball or even exercise. Mr. Fittanuff said we had to prepare our minds and bodies for THE TEST. We all learned something about meditating and about something called "yogurt." Like I said, things were getting pretty weird at school. I got to thinking THE TEST was sort of important.

Even my mom knew about THE TEST. When she read me my bedtime story, I had to complete a ditto and give the main idea before I could go to sleep.

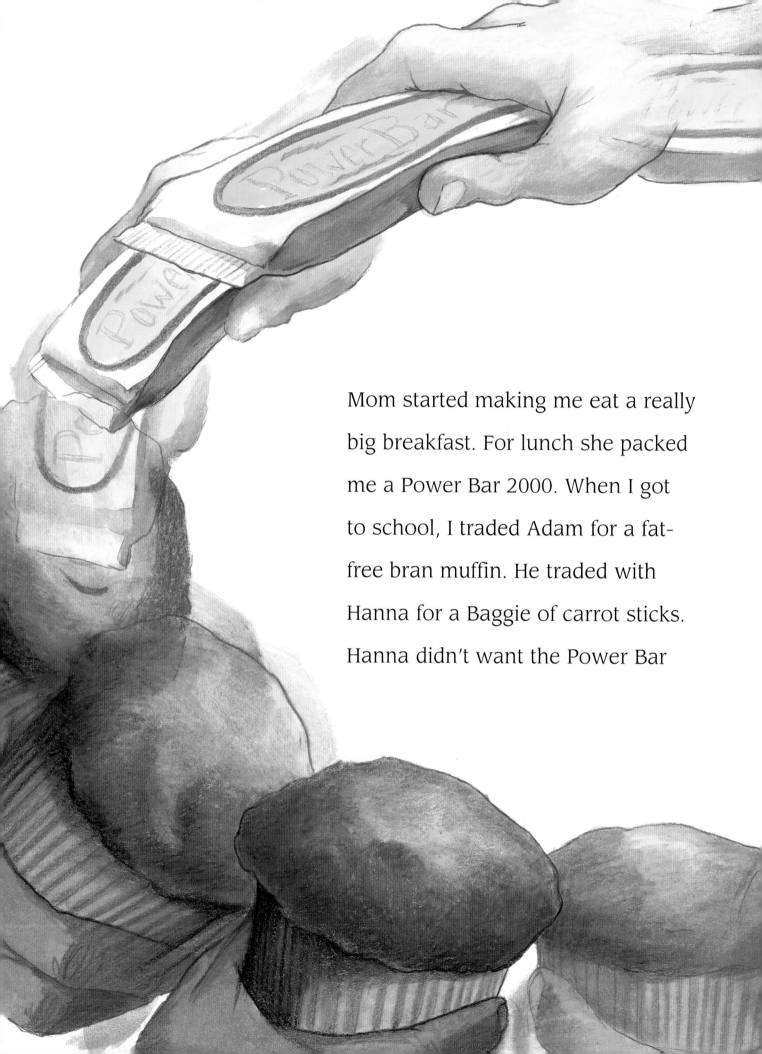

Mom started making me eat a really big breakfast. For lunch she packed me a Power Bar 2000. When I got to school, I traded Adam for a fat-free bran muffin. He traded with Hanna for a Baggie of carrot sticks. Hanna didn't want the Power Bar

so she asked her best friend, Meredith, if she would trade for her apple. Somehow someone must have wanted the apple, and I'm not sure what happened but I had the Power Bar 2000 again.

One night Mom took me to a PTA meeting. A man was there talking about THE TEST. He wasn't a teacher or a parent or even the principal, but whoever he was he seemed to think THE TEST was very important. So did the parents.

The day of THE TEST the janitor, Mr. Surley, closed off the whole hallway. You couldn't even walk down it unless you had a pass. And you had to whisper. Miss Malarkey had to whisper the secret password to Mr. Surley before she could go to Room 10.

That morning there were more teachers than kids waiting for the nurse.

Miss Malarkey's job was to hand out the No. 2 pencils and the scratch paper. She looked like she didn't get enough sleep. Principal Wiggins was keeping the time. We couldn't even touch THE TEST until he waved the flag. When it was time to start, he waved the flag so hard, something happened to his hair.

THE TEST took forever.
It took two whole
days. My friend Carmine
got in trouble for not
using his scratch paper
the right way. I thought
his ninja warrior looked
pretty good, though.

Miss Malarkey caught Barry with his
baseball cards.

Morgan got a stomachache and had to go to the nurse. The hall monitor gave her such a hard time, she threw up right in the hall.

When Miss Malarkey said to erase all your pencil marks, Janet erased her whole test.

Principal Wiggins was in the room for a while, but he had a stomachache and had to go to the nurse. I hope he didn't throw up in the hall too.

After THE TEST everybody got prizes and had treats and we got extra recess. Even Steven, who fell asleep two times during THE TEST. Miss Malarkey looked wiped out, and she didn't even take THE TEST.

It's been a long time since we took THE TEST. Things are back to normal. Principal Wiggins isn't yelling quite as much. The cafeteria lady started serving potato chips again. Mom's packing me good old peanut butter and jelly sandwiches. And Miss Malarkey is letting her fingernails grow real long. I guess THE TEST really wasn't that important after all.

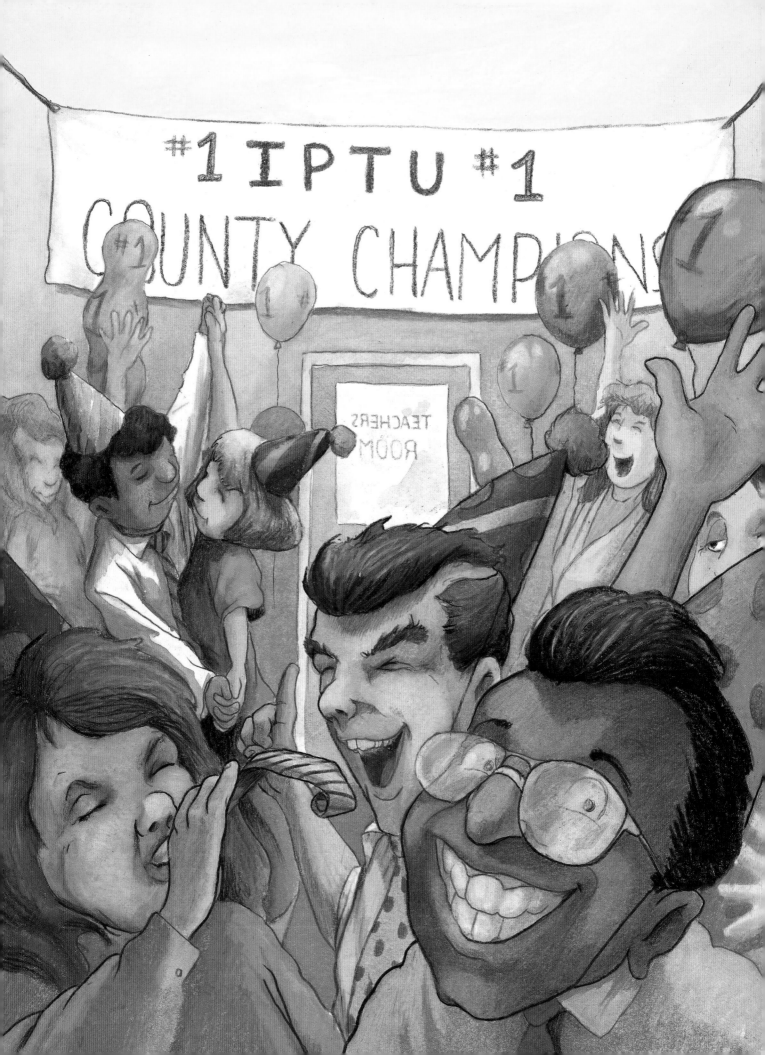